WELCOME TO PASSPORT TO READING

A beginning reader's ticket to a brand-new world!

Every book in this program is designed to build read-along and read-alone skills, level by level, through engaging and enriching stories. As the reader turns each page, he or she will become more confident with new vocabulary, sight words, and comprehension.

These PASSPORT TO READING levels will help you choose the perfect book for every reader.

READING TOGETHER
Read short words in simple sentence structures together to begin a reader's journey.

READING OUT LOUD
Encourage developing readers to sound out words in more complex stories with simple vocabulary.

READING INDEPENDENTLY
Newly independent readers gain confidence reading more complex sentences with higher word counts.

READY TO READ MORE
Readers prepare for chapter books with fewer illustrations and longer paragraphs.

This book features sight words from the educator-supported Dolch Sight Words List. This encourages the reader to recognize commonly used vocabulary words, increasing reading speed and fluency.

For more information, please visit passporttoreadingbooks.com.

Enjoy the journey!

Little, Brown and Company
Hachette Book Group
1290 Avenue of the Americas, New York, NY 10104
Visit us at LBYR.com
mylittlepony.com

First Edition: April 2019

Little, Brown and Company is a division of Hachette Book Group, Inc.
The Little, Brown name and logo are trademarks of Hachette Book Group, Inc.

The publisher is not responsible for websites (or their content) that are not owned by the publisher.

Library of Congress Control Number: 2018953128

ISBNs: 978-0-316-48684-2 (pbk.), 978-0-316-48683-5 (ebook),
978-0-316-48681-1 (ebook), 978-0-316-48682-8 (ebook)

Printed in the United States of America

CW

10 9 8 7 6 5 4 3 2 1

Passport to Reading titles are leveled by independent reviewers applying the standards developed by Irene Fountas and Gay Su Pinnell in *Matching Books to Readers: Using Leveled Books in Guided Reading*, Heinemann, 1999.

Licensed By:

Meet the
Squad!

by Celeste Sisler

L B

LITTLE, BROWN AND COMPANY

New York   Boston

Attention, My Little Pony fans!
Look for these words when you read this book.
Can you spot them all?

Flurry Heart

Unicorn

ribbons

Pegasus

Welcome to Ponyville!
Ponyville is a town in Equestria
where creatures big and small
learn about friendship.
My name is Starlight Glimmer!

These are my new friends,
Twilight Sparkle and the rest
of the Mane Six.

Let us meet them and see
how everypony is special
in their own way!

Princess Twilight Sparkle
is an Alicorn.

An Alicorn is a pony with
wings and a magical horn.

Twilight Sparkle was not
always a princess.
She used magic to help her friends,
and she saved the day!
That is how she became a princess.

Now Twilight lives in the
Castle of Friendship.
The School of Friendship
is next to the castle.

Her school teaches everycreature
the Magic of Friendship.
Twilight's best friends work
at her school, too.

 Twilight is happy to be an
aunt to baby Flurry Heart!
Twilight loves playing games
with Flurry Heart.

Flurry Heart is an Alicorn, too!
She lives in the Crystal Empire.
Flurry Heart's parents are
Princess Cadance and
Shining Armor.

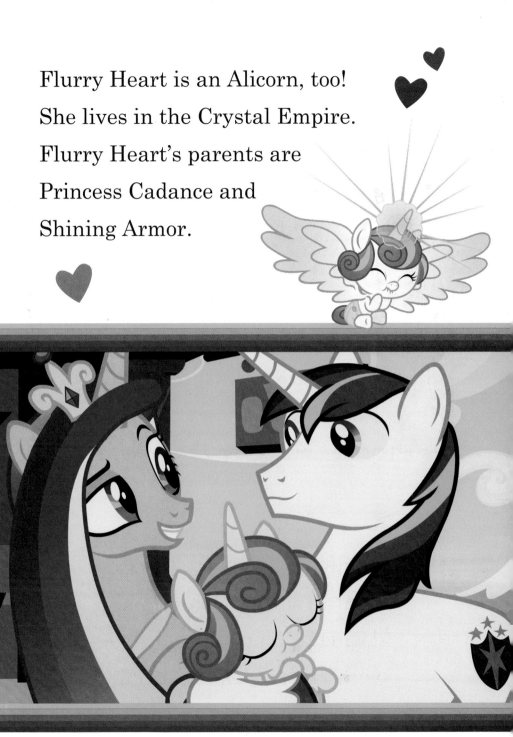

Twilight's best friend is Spike.

Spike is a Dragon who loves eating gems.

He lives in the Castle of Friendship

and has magical green fire breath!

The Mane Six can always count
on Spike to be brave and good.
Spike cares for all the ponies,
but he has a special crush on Rarity.

Rarity is a Unicorn.
She works and lives
in her Carousel Boutique.

Rarity is very bighearted.

She owns three shops where she designs

clothing that makes everypony sparkle.

She uses ribbons, buttons, and gemstones.

Rarity's cat, Opalescence,
also loves sparkly things.
Opalescence is not friendly
with most of the ponies,
but she likes Fluttershy.

Fluttershy is a Pegasus.
She lives in a small cottage
near the Everfree Forest
with her bunny, Angel.

Fluttershy takes care of all the animals
in Ponyville at her animal sanctuary.
She is kind and gentle.

Fluttershy thinks the best
of everycreature.
She has even made friends with
grumpy Manticores and big Dragons.

As a Pegasus, Fluttershy has wings. She can fly and walk on clouds. Rainbow Dash is a Pegasus, too!

Rainbow Dash loves flying!
She is the fastest pony in Ponyville.
She lives in her Cloudominium
with her pet tortoise, Tank.

Rainbow Dash is loyal.
She fixes the weather with
a fast kick or a flip.
She is proud to show off
her colorful Sonic Rainboom.

Rainbow Dash attended
Wonderbolt Academy and
became a member of the team!

When she is not flying,
Rainbow Dash loves
competing with Applejack.

Applejack lives and works at Sweet Apple Acres. She is part of the large Apple family.

Applejack is never afraid
to get her hooves dirty
and help anypony in need.
She is honest and strong.

Applejack's dog, Winona, loves
helping out on the farm, too.
Winona once helped round up
a pack of Pinkie Pies!

Pinkie Pie lives above
Sugarcube Corner
with her green gator,
Gummy.

29

Pinkie works at the bakery
with the Cake family.

Pinkie Pie loves to P-A-R-T-Y!
She knows how to cheer up anypony
with her party cannon or yummy treats.

Pinkie Pie also loves to sing
and make her friends laugh.
To Pinkie Pie, every day in
Ponyville is a day to celebrate!

Now you can celebrate how everypony is special in their own way!
You are always welcome in Ponyville.

Come back soon!
Love, Starlight Glimmer.